J F Up2U U71gno
Fields, Jan.
Ghost light burning

(Up2U Adventures)

GHOST LIGHT BURNING

by Jan Fields
illustrated by Valerio Fabbretti

Calico

An Imprint of Magic Wagon
www.abdopublishing.com

www.abdopublishing.com

Published by Magic Wagon, a division of ABDO, PO Box 398166, Minneapolis, Minnesota 55439. Copyright © 2015 by Abdo Consulting Group, Inc. International copyrights reserved in all countries. No part of this book may be reproduced in any form without written permission from the publisher. Calico™ is a trademark and logo of Magic Wagon.

Printed in the United States of America, North Mankato, Minnesota.
102014
012015

Written by Jan Fields
Illustrations by Valerio Fabbretti
Edited by Rochelle Baltzer, Heidi M. D. Elston, Bridget O'Brien
Cover and interior design by Laura Rask

Library of Congress Cataloging-in-Publication Data

Fields, Jan, author.
  Ghost light burning : an Up2U mystery adventure / by Jan Fields ; illustrated by Valerio Fabbretti.
      pages cm. -- (Up2U adventures)
  Summary: From the beginning Jack thinks there is something sinister about the old Dareville Community Theater, where his father is the new caretaker-- and that is before the ghost of the actor Victor Dare tells him he must solve the mystery of the actor's disappearance or be haunted forever.
  ISBN 978-1-62402-092-6
  1. Ghost stories. 2. Detective and mystery stories. 3. Plot-your-own stories. 4. Missing persons--Juvenile fiction. 5. Theaters--Juvenile fiction. 6. Actors- -Juvenile fiction. [1. Ghosts--Fiction. 2. Haunted places--Fiction. 3. Missing persons--Fiction. 4. Theaters--Fiction. 5. Actors and actresses--Fiction. 6. Mystery and detective stories. 7. Plot-your-own stories.] I. Fabbretti, Valerio, illustrator. II. Title.
  PZ7.F479177Gh 2015
  813.6--dc23
  [Fic]
                                                2014034274

TABLE OF CONTENTS

CHAPTER
→» 1 «←

Welcome to Dareville

Jack Watson stared up at the old brick building that loomed over him. The narrow windows at the front of the building were mostly broken. One was covered with warped plywood. Someone had spray-painted the outline of a cartoon ghost on the plywood. The sign over the doors read EVIL COMMUNITY THEATER.

His dad followed his gaze and chuckled. "Looks like the Dareville Community Theater could use a new sign."

"Among other things," Jack muttered, shifting the cardboard box of books in his arms.

"Look on the bright side," his dad urged. "I've got a job, and it comes with a place for us to stay."

Jack's dad was big on looking at the bright side in gloomy situations. Jack preferred to look on the reality side. As bad as the old building looked, it was probably worse inside.

He sometimes wondered why his dad couldn't get a job looking after a mansion. Jack imagined spending the summer before fifth grade splashing in a private pool. He would sit in a poolside chair and reread his favorite mysteries while sipping cold lemonade. A job like that would be all bright side. You wouldn't even have to look for it.

They trudged to the stage door, where his dad fiddled with the old locks. Jack stepped up to a window near the door. A thin board covered part of the window, but Jack could see glass behind it. He tried to make out shapes in the dark interior.

Just as Jack's dad coaxed the lock to turn and pulled open the door, sudden movement flashed by the window. Jack jumped back with a shout. He tripped over his own feet and fell on his rear. His box landed beside him and split open, spilling books out on the cracked pavement.

"Are you all right?" his dad asked as he bent to pile Jack's books back into the torn box.

"Something moved inside."

Jack and his dad looked toward the open door. Sunlight spilled into the room beyond, revealing an old wooden crate and a lot of dust. The thick dust showed no sign of footprints.

"Some of the windows are broken," his dad said. "Maybe a stray cat got in."

"I don't think so," Jack said.

His dad scratched his head. "Maybe it was a trick of the light as I opened the door."

"Maybe." Yet Jack was certain it wasn't light or a cat. It was a person.

Someone was in the old theater. Someone tall and thin and *fast*.

Jack didn't bother arguing with his dad. He gathered the rest of his books and followed his dad inside the old theater.

"I'll need to check out the whole building for safety," his dad said. "But let's get you settled in the apartment first."

The dim light from the windows lit the way to a set of wooden stairs. "The apartment is on the basement level," Jack's dad said. The stairs groaned under their feet with each step. When they reached the bottom, his dad used the light from his cell phone to find a switch.

Jack heard the click of the switch but the darkness never lifted. Several more clicks followed, then a sigh. "There must be something wrong with the lights. I'll check the fuses. You can wait in the apartment. There's a lantern."

Jack followed the firefly glow of his dad's phone through what felt like a maze. The air felt thick and faintly damp. The thick coating of dust made the wood floor soft and slippery under Jack's sneakers.

Finally his dad flung open a door. "Here we are. I'll have the lantern lit in just a second."

The cheer in his dad's voice sounded forced. It was tough to look on the bright side when you stood in the pitch dark. After some rustling and the striking of a match, light finally glowed from the lantern that rested on the kitchen table.

Jack looked around the shadowy room. A couple of straight wooden chairs, some battered counters, a rattling fridge, an old stove, and a rusty sink completed the apartment's kitchen.

He looked into the living room. A sofa slouched across from an old television perched on milk crates. His dad pointed at a pair of narrow doors. "That one leads to the bathroom and the other one leads to your bedroom. The sofa folds out. That's where I'll sleep. You can take the lantern and go check out your room. I'll deal with the fuse box."

His dad headed out, whistling in the dark.

Jack set his box on the table and picked up the lantern. He decided to stay right where he was. He'd read enough mysteries to know that bad things happened as soon as you started wandering off on your own. On the wall above the sofa, a huge mirror reflected the room. Jack stepped closer and looked into the mirror.

His glasses were smeared and his black hair was streaked with dust, making him look like the creepy theater was turning him into an old man. He leaned closer to the mirror to look at a smudge on his cheek. That's when he saw the pale figure step up behind him and smile.

CHAPTER
→ 2 ←

The Great Victor Dare

Jack shrieked and spun around. The room was empty except for Jack and a few floating cobwebs. He turned back to the mirror, and only his own face peered at him. The door from the hallway creaked open and Jack yelled again.

"Jack?" Light spilled in from the hallway as his dad walked in with a box full of cleaning supplies. "Are you all right?"

Jack cleared his throat. "Fine."

"I fixed the fuses." His dad pulled the string hanging from the light over the kitchen table. The light was still dim, as if the effort of pushing back the shadows was too much. "I know this old place can make you jumpy, but you'll get used to it. You'll see."

Jack considered telling his dad about the man in the mirror, but he knew his dad would think he imagined it.

"How did you like your room?" his dad asked as he began cleaning the kitchen.

"I haven't checked yet." Jack picked up his cardboard box and carried it into the small bedroom. The dim ceiling light left plenty of shadows.

Every inch of the bedroom walls were covered with theater posters. Posters were layered over posters until some only showed bits and pieces. A glaring eye peered from between two posters advertising musicals. In another spot, a sagging poster revealed the word *beware* behind it.

Jack froze. Fear stuck in his throat like half-chewed bread as he stared at one of the posters. A thin man with a hawk nose and a moustache glared down at him. A white scarf fluttered around the man's neck. The actor's name was printed in big letters: Victor Dare.

Jack recognized that face. It was the one from the mirror.

He backed out of the bedroom, somehow unwilling to turn away from the piercing eyes. "Dad? Have you ever heard of Victor Dare?"

His dad looked at him over the open fridge door. "Sure. He was the closest thing Dareville had to a star. Thirty years ago, the old guy disappeared one night from the middle of the stage during a show."

"What happened to him?"

His dad shrugged, before turning back to the fridge. "He never turned up. It's a big mystery."

Jack sat in one of the kitchen chairs. "Did anyone ever think the theater was haunted?"

His dad chuckled. "Every empty building is supposed to be haunted. But I think the only things haunting this one are cobwebs and mice."

His head popped back up behind the fridge door. "By the way, I didn't see any sign of a cat when I fixed the fuses and brought in the cleaning supplies." His dad rested his forearms on the fridge door and smiled. "Speaking of cleaning, how about you pitch in and help?"

Together Jack and his dad scrubbed, dusted, and mopped until the apartment only looked worn, instead of dirty. After the hard work, Jack yawned his way through a late supper. "Let's go make up your bed," his dad said. "Then I'll pop out to check all the doors and windows."

Jack didn't really want to stay in the apartment alone, but he didn't want to look like a big chicken either. He helped his dad make up the bed. The room looked much better with the bright quilt and pillows.

"I'll be back in a wink," his dad said as he headed back out the door.

Jack noticed his box of books was empty. The mysteries sat in neat rows on the cheap bookcase that doubled as a side table next to the bed. He wondered when his dad did that. Jack hadn't seen him come back into the bedroom while they cleaned.

Just then, a voice spoke close to Jack's ear. "So, you are a lad who loves mysteries?"

Jack whirled around, expecting to face an empty room again. Instead, the man from the theater poster stood next to the bedroom door. He wore a long coat just as he had in the poster, though he had no scarf.

Jack could see right through the man's pale face. "Y-y-you're Victor Dare's ghost?" he stuttered.

"I prefer the word *specter.*" The man swept a finger across his transparent moustache. "*Ghost* sounds so ordinary. I was never ordinary. I was a star."

Jack waited to see if the ghost was going to rattle chains or rush at him. Instead, he merely walked across the room to pose under his poster. Jack edged toward the door.

"You're not going to run away, are you?" Dare asked, raising one eyebrow.

Jack froze. "Did you want something?"

"Well, my young detective, I would like you to solve the mystery of my disappearance."

"How can you not know that already?" Jack asked.

"I have no memory of that night after I delivered my stirring lines." Dare drew himself up tall and straight. Suddenly, bits and pieces of the posters ripped themselves from the walls in a storm of tattered paper. When the last torn piece settled on the floor, only the posters featuring Victor Dare remained. "I have played all the greatest heroes and detectives in literary history, but I don't know the answer to this one mystery."

"What if I can't figure it out?"

The ghost drifted closer to Jack and smiled wide. "Then you'll need to get used to being haunted, my boy, because I'm sticking with you until you do."

CHAPTER
→ 3 ←

Midnight Meeting

After demanding Jack's promise of help, the ghost vanished. Jack swept up the bits of torn poster and carried them out to the kitchen trash. He buried them under dirty paper towels so his dad wouldn't see them. He was pretty sure part of the caretaker job included not letting anyone tear up old theater posters.

Jack figured he wouldn't get much sleep with Victor Dare staring down at him from every wall. It felt as if he'd barely crawled under the covers before someone was shaking him awake. He opened his eyes to see the ghost's white face glowing in the darkness.

Jack opened his mouth to scream, but the ghost slapped a white hand over his mouth. "Please, don't shout," the ghost said. "We don't want to wake your father. Plus, I don't care for the noise."

Jack nodded and the ghost removed his hand. Jack frowned. "Why can't I see through you anymore?"

Dare smiled and spoke in a hollow voice. "Do you not know that tonight, when the clock strikes midnight, all the evil things in the world will have full sway?"

"What?"

"That's a quote from a writer named Bram Stoker. He wrote *Dracula*." The ghost tugged at the sleeves of his jacket. "I'm not an evil thing, but it's the closest quote I know, and it *is* midnight."

"No one gets up at midnight," Jack complained.

"I do. Now come along. It's time to investigate. We will start at the scene of the crime."

"I can't leave the apartment," Jack whispered fiercely. "My dad would freak out."

"Then we will not tell him."

Jack didn't have an answer for that. It was clear the ghost wasn't leaving. He followed the glowing figure out of the apartment and onto the huge stage.

The heavy velvet stage drapes were thick with dust and rotten from dampness and time. The stage itself groaned with Jack's every step. A single light burned in the middle of the stage. "At least we have a light," Jack said.

"It is the ghost light," Dare said.

"Someone knew this place had a ghost?" Jack asked.

"All theaters have ghosts. The ghost light is an old tradition. It lights the stage for ghosts who may wish to perform." Dare smiled his sharp-toothed smile again. "It is not a good idea to anger ghosts."

The dim light wasn't nearly enough to show much in the deep darkness of the theater. "I don't know what I'm going to find in the dark," Jack said.

The ghost tapped his moustache with one finger. "An ace detective would have brought a flashlight."

Jack was sure an ace detective wouldn't let a ghost tell him what to do either. "Just show me where you were standing."

The ghost crossed to the center of the stage. His shoes made no sound as he walked. Jack followed him. The floor was thick with dust and scattered bits of torn curtain. It was hard to imagine what it must have looked like on the night the actor disappeared.

"What were you doing when you disappeared?"

"Saying my lines, of course," the ghost said. "I was playing the second greatest detective in literary history. I consider Sherlock Holmes to be the first."

Jack nodded. Sherlock Holmes was his favorite, too. "Who were you playing?"

The ghost smiled and tugged on his moustache. "Hercule Poirot." He tilted his head to one side and spoke with an accent. "It is the brain, the little gray cells on which one must rely. One must seek the truth within--not without."

Jack wrinkled his nose. "You solve a mystery with clues, not just by thinking a lot."

"You never know," the ghost said. "We may need both for this mystery. Would you like to try standing where I stood? Perhaps you'll see a clue."

"Of course," Jack said. He wished he'd thought of that. The ghost moved out of the way. Jack took the spot at the center of the stage. He looked out toward the rows of seats that would have held the audience. They were just dark blobs. He looked up and saw more dark shapes. "What's up there?"

"All sorts of catwalks," the ghost said.

"The theater had cats?" asked Jack.

The ghost shook his head and muttered about working with children. Then he cleared his throat and said, "Catwalks are narrow walkways that give stagehands access to things like lights and pulleys. Once our company performed *Peter Pan* and ropes from the catwalks allowed the actors to fly."

Jack looked at the ghost in surprise. "You played Peter Pan?"

The ghost looked insulted. "Peter Pan was played by a young woman. I played Captain Hook!"

"Do you think someone could have thrown down a rope lasso and pulled you up off the stage?"

"That's not how it's done. There are harnesses and such when one flies in the theater. And everyone in the audience would have seen that."

That made sense. So if the actor didn't disappear by going up, what if he disappeared by going down? "What's under here?" Jack asked, stomping hard on the stage.

Suddenly a trapdoor opened up directly beneath him, dropping Jack into the total darkness below.

CHAPTER
→ 4 ←

The Search for Clues

As the stage dropped out from under him, Jack flailed his arms. His fingers struck the edge of the hole, and he grabbed on. He dangled above darkness so thick he had no idea what he would find at the bottom. "Help!"

The ghost stepped up to the hole's edge. The glowing tips of his shoes were inches from Jack's fingers. For a moment, Jack was sure the ghost intended to stomp his fingers. "Help!"

The ghost bent way over looking more like a hawk than ever as he peered at Jack. "Can you climb back up?"

"No," Jack said.

His fingers ached, and the muscles in his arms trembled. "And I don't know how long I can hold on."

"I wonder what time it is," the ghost said.

"Who cares?" Jack yelled. "Help me, please!"

The ghost stepped off the edge of the stage and floated down, snagging Jack around the waist along the way. They floated to the floor below. When his feet touched the ground, Jack felt the ghost's arm slip out from around him. Jack's legs still felt wobbly, but he managed to stay on them.

"What happened?" he asked.

"You fell through the trapdoor."

"You might have mentioned a trapdoor earlier!" Jack yelled. "Are you trying to get me killed?"

The ghost frowned at him. "Not at all. Having been killed, I don't recommend it to anyone."

Jack took a deep breath to help him calm down. "Have you realized that we've solved the mystery? You fell through the trapdoor. That's how you disappeared."

"That trapdoor doesn't simply open during a play performance," the ghost said.

"It certainly did tonight."

"Yes. It must be broken," the ghost said. He rubbed his moustache with one finger as he looked around the dark area under the stage. "There should be a lift."

"A lift?" Jack echoed.

The ghost nodded. "The lift is like a portable elevator. It allows people to appear and disappear from the stage."

"That must be what happened," Jack said. "Someone moved the lift, and you fell through the trapdoor."

"I don't remember. But that wouldn't be disappearing. I would have been lying on the floor down here."

"That's true," Jack said. "I wish we had more light. It's hard to search for clues when you can't see."

The ghost snapped his fingers and the weak electric lights under the stage snapped on. Then the ghost led Jack to the lift. "This should be under the stage, not way over here."

Jack saw something on the floor and knelt beside the lift. A pale scarf barely peeked out from under the lift deck. Jack tugged it out and held it up. It was exactly like the scarf the actor wore in all the posters on the walls in his bedroom.

"A clue!" the ghost cried. "Sherlock Holmes would be proud of you. But the real key to a clue is what you make of it. You must ask yourself the question: Does the scarf mean anything to the greater mystery?"

Jack grinned. "The little things are infinitely the most important."

The ghost laughed and patted Jack on the back. "A quote from Sherlock himself. You *are* a reader. So what does it mean?"

"You wore it in every poster, so it was obviously important to you."

"It was my trademark!" The ghost waved his hand dramatically.

"But you're not wearing it now. It means you were down here, you lost it, and you never had time to find it again," Jack said. He leaned down to look at the lift deck. "I think we need to raise this. If your scarf was under it, something else could be as well. Do you know how this lift works?"

"Of course!" The ghost looped the newly found scarf around his neck and walked around to the crank wheel that raised and lowered the lift. He pushed against the handle, but nothing moved. The ghost looked down at his hands. "It must be after one o'clock.

I no longer have the strength that I had. I cannot move the crank."

"Let me try." Jack threw his weight behind the crank but it was stuck. He struggled until he was sweaty from the effort. Finally he gave up. "Maybe we can come back tomorrow night when you're strong again."

"Good plan," the ghost said.

Jack looked around the room and spotted a pair of black gloves with fancy red stitching sticking out of a pile of wooden crates. He pointed in that direction. "Are these yours too?"

The ghost sniffed. "Hardly. I always wore white gloves so the audience could see my every movement. I was known for my dramatic hand gestures."

"Right," Jack said. "They still might be important." Jack crossed the room to tug on the gloves. At first they seemed stuck in the crack between crates. Then they came loose so suddenly that Jack fell over backward. The tall stack of crates swayed above him.

Jack scrambled as the crates toppled over and fell.

CHAPTER
→» 5 «←

An Unlikely Help

Jack rolled into a ball and put his hands over his head. The crates crashed around him, exploding as they hit the floor. Bits of wood smacked against Jack, making him yelp.

Finally, quiet settled over the theater again. Jack sat up and coughed from the dust in the air. He moved his arms and legs, feeling the pains from the falling wood. Then he stood carefully. He couldn't believe he was still in one piece.

He looked around for the ghost, but he was nowhere in sight. Instead, Jack spotted his dad racing toward him. "Jack!"

"I'm all right," Jack said.

"What are you doing?" his dad yelled. "It's the middle of the night! Why are you down here climbing on the crates?"

"I wasn't climbing . . . ," Jack started to say.

But his dad talked over him as he checked him for broken bones. Finally he seemed to wind down. His voice turned from angry to tired and disappointed. "What were you doing?" he asked.

Jack shrugged. He didn't think his dad would believe Jack's ghostly experience. "I couldn't sleep. I wanted to look around."

"That will have to wait until I check out the whole theater," his dad said. "I'll let you know the places you can play."

Jack wasn't really interested in playing in the creepy building. But he didn't say that either. Instead he gestured at the piles of splintered wood around him. "Can I help clean up?"

His dad shook his head. "Go on back to bed. I'll clean up here and be along soon."

Jack headed back to the apartment. He wished he could tell his dad what really happened, but mostly he wished they'd never come to the old theater. When he slammed his bedroom door behind him, he shouted, "Thanks for almost getting me killed."

If the ghost heard him, he didn't bother to respond.

The next morning, Jack sat across from his dad at the shaky table in the kitchen. Silence stretched between them until Jack said, "Dad? Do you believe in ghosts?"

His dad had been staring into his coffee mug. He jumped at Jack's voice. "Ghosts? No." His eyes widened. "Is that why you were wandering around last night? Were you looking for ghosts?"

Jack shook his head. *Not exactly*, he thought.

His dad sighed. "I know this old place is creepy, but don't let your imagination run away, okay?"

"Yeah, sure."

His dad gave him an apologetic smile. "I'm sorry I yelled last night. The accident just scared me."

It didn't do much for me either, Jack thought.

"I'm sorry, too," Jack said.

His dad nodded. "Why don't you get out of this old place for a while? There's a nice park at the end of the block."

"Actually, I thought I might go to the library."

His dad smiled again. "More mystery books? Sure, that will be fine. I'm going to make sure there aren't any more dangerous spots in the theater."

"Be careful on the stage," Jack said. "The trapdoor is broken."

"How do you know that?" Then his dad shook his head and held up one hand. "No, don't tell me. I can worry enough without the details. I'll check it out. Thanks. Have a good time at the library."

In the bright sunshine outside, Jack's experience with the ghost suddenly seemed like a dream. Who could believe in ghosts on a sunny day in June? He looked up at the theater. In daylight, it looked old and sad instead of creepy. Maybe he could just forget about the ghost stuff.

Jack crossed the weed-spotted parking lot to the sidewalk. Next door, a broken-down house leaned into the theater, as if keeping an eye on the place. Judging by the thickly overgrown yard, Jack assumed the house was as empty as the theater. Then the front gate creaked open. An old woman in black limped out.

"You!" she said, pointing a crooked finger at him.

Jack stopped and tried to look helpful. The woman's face was pale and lined. Her snow white hair was pulled back into a tight bun, and she peered at him through thick glasses. "That theater is dangerous!"

"It is in pretty bad shape," Jack agreed.

The woman shook her head. She shuffled closer and grabbed Jack's arm. "No. You don't understand. There's evil in there. It wants you dead!"

CHAPTER
→» 6 «←

Death Trap

Jack stared down at the bony fingers clinging to his arm. "Do you mean the ghost?" he asked.

The old woman frowned and let go of his arm. "I am talking about dark forces. They will get you as they have gotten the others."

"Others?" Jack yelped. "Do you mean Victor Dare? Do you know what happened to him? I'm trying to find out how he disappeared."

The woman shook her head. "No. No. Questions only put you in more danger. You must leave the theater."

"I'd like that," Jack said. "But my dad is the caretaker. He's not going to leave."

The woman moaned, putting her hands to her head. "You are just a boy. I cannot let you become like the others. What can I do?"

"Hey, it's all right," Jack said. "I'll find out what happened to Victor Dare. Then he'll stop haunting the theater. No more dark forces, right?"

She wailed again.

Jack's eyes darted up and down the street. He didn't want anyone to see him talking to the strange woman. They might think he'd done something bad to make her wail like that. "Hey, maybe you could give me some tips. You know, advice on how to deal with the dark forces?"

She looked up at him sharply, her eyes narrowed. Then she nodded. She reached into a deep pocket of her black skirt and pulled out a slender can of salt. "You must use this," she said. "Spirits cannot stand salt."

Jack looked at the can she held in her trembling hand. Salt? As ghost busting tools went, that was kind of disappointing. At least the woman wasn't wailing anymore. "I will," he said as he took the salt. "Thanks. I have to go now."

Jack stuffed the can into the pocket of the sleeveless hoodie he wore. Then he hurried down the sidewalk.

"Beware!" the woman called after him.

Jack nodded and waved, walking even faster. He didn't slow down until he was inside the library. He stood at the front desk, panting slightly and waiting for his eyes to adjust from being outside.

"I like to see a young man panting for knowledge."

Jack turned to the smiling librarian behind the desk. "I'm looking for information about the old theater and Victor Dare." He was ready to trot out a story about a school summer project, but the librarian didn't ask. She just showed him how to access the old newspaper files on a computer in the local history reading room.

"We had everything digitized about five years ago," the librarian said. "You can use the search feature to find what you want. Happy reading!"

Jack quickly learned the actor's disappearance was big news when it happened. He found letters to the editor filled with theories, ranging from practical to crazy. Some people thought the disappearance was a publicity stunt to save the failing theater.

One guy thought Dare was taken by aliens.

Jack brought up the actual news story about the disappearance and began reading:

Dareville's Star Actor Vanishes

Emily Manning, who sat in the front row of the audience, described Dare's disappearance. "He finished his line and waved his hands. Then he vanished in a puff of smoke."

In the grand theater tradition, Dare's understudy, Felix Marshall, rushed onstage to finish the play. "It was my finest performance," Marshall told reporters. "I showed that I'm a better actor than Dare ever hoped to be. I hope to lead this theater company to true greatness. Dare's hammy acting has only been holding us back."

When questioned about the possibility of Dare's disappearance being a publicity stunt, theater owner George Brass said, "The loss of our star certainly cannot help Dareville Community Theater in any way. I doubt we'll do another show here."

Police conducted a search of the theater building. No trace of the missing actor turned up. The disappearance remains a mystery.

Jack did a few more searches but only came up with a small notice of the theater's official closing. The notice said the performers would be moving on to other theater groups. He searched for more information about Felix Marshall, but didn't find anything. *I guess he never did lead anyone to true greatness*, Jack thought.

As he sat back in his chair, his stomach growled loudly. He hopped up and headed back to the theater, hoping there was something good in the old fridge for lunch.

When Jack got back to the apartment, he wasn't surprised to find it empty. He made a cheese and mayo sandwich and sat at the rickety table to eat and think. He wondered what the detectives from his books would do next. He had done his research. He'd looked for clues at the scene of the crime. What was the next step?

Jack decided to search the actor's dressing room. He climbed the steps to the main floor and headed backstage. Then he froze in his tracks. He heard moaning up ahead. Jack slowly walked toward the sound and found a broken pile of theater flats.

An arm stuck out from the pile of flats. The fingers twitched as the person buried under the flats moaned again. It was his dad!

CHAPTER
→» 7 «←

Cracking the Case

"Dad!" Jack yelled as he searched for something to move the heavy flats. He heard his dad call his name and yelled, "Hold on! I'll get you out!"

Jack flung open wide double doors marked Property Room. Inside he saw tables and chairs, swords and shields, and telephones and typewriters. Everything a theater might ever use seemed stuffed into the large room. Somewhere Jack was sure to find something to move the heavy props.

He raced back with one of the long swords, but quickly saw he needed something much longer and stronger. He dug amongst the pool cues, jousting lances, and long wooden spears. Finally he found a sturdy wooden pole. Jack used it as a lever to lift the flats and shove them to one side. His dad called out encouragement as Jack worked.

Jack saw that most of the flats had landed against one another as they tumbled over. This kept the bulk of the weight from hitting his dad. Only one rested directly on him at the bottom of the pile. When Jack moved it, his dad crawled free.

Jack helped his dad to his feet. "Are you all right?" Jack gasped as he saw a trickle of blood run down his dad's arm. "You're bleeding!"

His dad pulled a clean handkerchief from his pocket and pressed it to his arm. "I think the flat that landed on me had a nail sticking out. I better go over to the clinic for a tetanus shot." He smiled at Jack and threw an arm around him. "I was more stuck than anything. I couldn't reach my cell phone. I don't know what I would have done without you."

His dad limped beside Jack on the way out of the theater. "Why do you think the flats fell?" Jack asked.

His dad shook his head. "I don't know. They looked fine when I went by them earlier. I don't like this. I shouldn't have brought you into this. I'm going to have to call the owner. This job is more dangerous than I was told."

By the time they got to the clinic, the bleeding had stopped, but Jack's dad was feeling all his bruises and bumps. The doctor gave him a shot and some pain medicine. "You should be more careful," the doctor said. "Those bruises could have been breaks. What happened anyway?"

Jack's dad explained about the theater flats, and the doctor frowned. "I'm surprised that old theater is still standing. You'd think it would be worth more if they tore it down and built something useful there. At any rate, you get some rest."

"I will," said Jack's dad.

The limping walk back to the theater seemed to take a lot out of Jack's dad. He took some of the medicine and lay down on the couch in the apartment. "You stay close by," he told Jack, his voice already thick with sleepiness. "I'll call the owner when I wake up. I think they might have to get someone else for this job. I don't care if I did sign a contract. Let him sue me."

Jack watched his dad sleep for a moment. Two accidents so close together seemed really suspicious. He wondered if the old lady was right. Were dark forces trying to hurt them? Would it be enough to leave the theater?

Victor Dare had promised to haunt him for a long time if he didn't solve the mystery. Jack didn't want the ghost following them when they left. He just wanted it all to stop.

He decided he better solve the mystery—and fast!

Jack wrote his dad a quick note and slipped out of the apartment. He would stick with the plan he had before he found his dad. He'd search Victor Dare's dressing room for clues. When Jack returned to the backstage area, he scrambled over the scattered theater flats and quickly found the dressing room with the star on the door.

Jack was surprised to see the dressing room was the cleanest place in the whole theater. Everything was neat. No dust lay on the dressing table or the mirror. It looked as if Victor Dare might return at any moment.

Jack sat in the chair facing the mirror. He flipped a switch, and the bulbs around the mirror flickered and lit up. The dressing table held little pots of makeup and sponges, as well as brushes and combs.

Jack picked up a tiny comb and turned it over in his hand. It would take forever to comb someone's hair with such a tiny comb. Then he spotted a can of moustache wax. He realized the comb was probably for Dare's moustache.

Beside the dressing table, a small end table held a pile of play scripts and two bound books. A volume of Sherlock Holmes stories lay under a thick book of Shakespeare's plays. Jack picked up the mystery stories and flipped through it. A slip of paper fell out from between the pages and fluttered to the floor.

Jack bent to pick up the paper. He stared at it for a long moment in shock. He finally knew the answer to the mystery of Victor Dare's disappearance.

The Ending Is Up2U!

If you believe Victor Dare's accident was really murder, turn to page 53.

→» OR «←

If you believe Victor Dare's accident was really a trick, turn to page 62.

→» OR «←

If you believe Victor Dare's accident was really an accident, turn to page 71.

ENDING

→» 1 «←

The Murder Uncovered

The newspaper photo in Jack's hand showed two actors grinning stiffly at the camera. The men stood ramrod straight with their bodies turned away from one another. They were not friends.

The tiny print at the bottom of the photo identified the men as Victor Dare and Felix Marshall. Though Jack had never seen Marshall before, he recognized his black leather gloves with the unusual stitching. Those gloves were at the scene of Dare's accident. Jack was certain Marshall had been there, too.

Jack carefully folded the newspaper photo and slipped it into his pocket. He needed to get those gloves.

As he walked through the dusty halls to the steps, Jack had a crawling feeling on the back of his neck. Someone was watching him. "Dare?" he yelled. No one answered.

He started down the creaky stairs. They seemed to groan more than usual. In fact, they were even swaying! Jack raced for the bottom of the stairs as they ripped away from the wall. The whole staircase bucked and twisted under his feet. He stumbled down another couple of steps, and then dove for the floor below. Behind him, the stairs finally collapsed in a heap of broken boards and dust.

Coughing, Jack looked up at the second floor. There was no way to get back up there now. The theater only had the one set of stairs to the basement.

Jack looked down the hall toward the under stage area. Should he go after the gloves or get his dad? Since his dad hadn't come running, Jack guessed he was still sleeping from the medicine. He decided to get the gloves. His dad might be awake after that.

As he scrambled over the piles of boards to reach the hall beyond, they shifted and slapped at his legs. He nearly fell down several times before he finally made it through.

At the spot where the crates collapsed, his dad had used bits of the broken crates to build a large corral for all the pieces, getting them safely out of the way. Jack looked around the area but didn't see any sign of the gloves.

The trapdoor to the stage still yawned open, but he had no way to reach it. Finally he climbed over the side of the wooden corral to pick among the broken crates for the gloves.

A high-pitched nasal voice shouted at him. "What do you think you're doing?"

Jack spun to face another ghost hovering just outside the wooden corral. He recognized the face from the photo in his pocket. "Felix Marshall," he said.

The ghost smirked. "The same. There's nothing in that box that belongs to you. You should come out while you can."

"There is something in here that belongs to you," Jack said in triumph when he saw a bit of leather under one of the boards. He snatched up the gloves and showed them to the ghost. "Your gloves. You wore them when you rigged the trapdoor to open under Victor Dare."

"I didn't mean to kill the old ham. I just wanted to wish him some theater luck and break his leg. It's a grand tradition you know. How was I to know he'd break his neck instead?"

"How did you get rid of the body?"

"You ask too many questions." The ghost crossed his arms and glared. His eyes had been bulging in the photo, but now they seemed ready to pop completely out of his head. The thought made Jack's skin crawl. "They always ask too many questions."

"They?" asked Jack.

"The caretakers." The ghost saw Jack's look of surprise and giggled. "You can't think you were the only *detective* Dare ever haunted? He talked every caretaker into this silly hunt. You just came a little closer to the answer than the others. But you'll meet the same end, I'm afraid."

The ghost waved his hand and the boards in the bin began bucking, knocking Jack around as they slapped at his body and head. Jack yelped and threw an arm over his head. He flung himself at the side of the corral as more boards slapped at him.

"Use the salt!"

Jack was startled by the shout from above. He looked up at the hole in the stage. The woman he'd met on the street looked back. "The salt," she repeated. "Use it on the ghost, boy!"

Jack shoved his hand into the kangaroo pocket of his hoodie and was surprised to find the can of salt was still in there. Jack pulled the top open and flung a stream of salt crystals at the ghost.

Everywhere the salt hit the glowing ghost, holes opened up and steamed thick vapor. The ghost shrieked and vanished. The wood in the corral with Jack stopped moving. Jack quickly scrambled out.

He ran to the spot directly under the hole. "The stairs collapsed," he told the woman. "I can't get out. Can you get help?"

The woman shook her head. "You'll need to get yourself out. Move the lift. You can use it to reach the stage."

Jack raced to the big lift and shoved against it. It didn't move at all. He pushed again, harder and harder.

"Hurry!" the woman shouted. "The ghost won't stay gone."

Jack slipped between the wall and the lift. He braced his back against the wall and lifted his legs to push. The lift moved bare inches. He pushed harder. The lift crept a little more.

"No you don't!"

The ghost of Felix Marshall appeared next to Jack. He waved a hand and the lift began to shove itself toward Jack. It was going to squash him against the wall! Jack pushed back with his legs, but he couldn't fight the terrible pressure.

"Get away from that boy!"

Jack recognized Victor Dare's voice. The pressure from the lift stopped and the lift dragged itself away from Jack. Jack staggered out to find the ghosts face-to-face. "You can't beat me," Marshall said. "You never could."

"Not alone," Dare bellowed. "But I'm not alone anymore."

Suddenly the space around Dare was full of ghosts. They were all men in work clothes. "My detectives. Get him, men."

The ghosts swarmed Marshall, pressing closer and closer to him until they were one glowing column. Then they turned around and around like a drill, until they had burrowed themselves deep below the theater. Victor Dare looked up at the smiling woman. "Emily. As beautiful as ever."

She smiled back, and the years seemed to fall away until she *was* beautiful. Then they both simply vanished.

Once Jack's dad woke up, he helped Jack move the lift to get them out of the theater. Under the lift, they found a hole in the floor filled with bones. The mystery of Victor Dare's disappearance was solved.

Jack even got his photo in the newspaper. It was a strange photo. Some trick of the light almost made it look like someone stood in the shadows behind Jack, a man with a hawk nose, a moustache, and a dashing pose.

ENDING
→» 2 «←
Tricky Bits

The store receipt in Jack's hand was barely two years old and seemed to be mostly for a bunch of mirrors. Though Jack couldn't imagine why a past caretaker would want to buy so many mirrors, the receipt itself wasn't that strange. The strange part was the note scrawled across the back. It was a quote from *The Hound of the Baskervilles*, Jack's favorite Sherlock Holmes story. The handwriting on the note matched the handwriting on all the other notes pasted to Victor Dare's mirror.

Jack read the quote aloud in a soft whisper, "The world is full of obvious things which nobody by any chance ever observes."

The obvious thing stared him right in the face. Ghosts don't go shopping, yet this receipt had Dare's handwriting on it. He'd disappeared thirty years before, but never stopped shopping?

"Great detective I am," Jack muttered. He shoved the receipt into the pocket of his sleeveless hoodie, right next to the salt. The woman had given him the salt for the ghosts. But there were no ghosts. Jack shook his head again.

He looked around the room with a fresh eye. Now he knew why the room was so clean. Ghosts don't clean dressing rooms, but a picky old actor might. Since there wasn't a bed or kitchen in the dressing room, there must be another place Dare was using as his hiding spot.

Jack thought back to the night when he'd tried to raise the lift platform. He'd needed help, but the ghost was suddenly too weak. Only Dare wasn't a ghost, so why didn't he help Jack raise the platform? Something must lie underneath that Dare didn't want revealed.

Jack was certain he'd found an important clue, but he needed help. He raced for the apartment to get his dad. His dad was still asleep on the sofa, snoring softly. "Dad!" Jack shouted, shaking his father's shoulder. "I solved the mystery, but I need your help."

His dad made some sleepy grumbling noises but didn't open his eyes. Jack shook him again, but got even fewer sleepy grumbles the second time. His dad wasn't going to wake up until he'd slept off the medicine.

"Terrific," Jack muttered. "How do I move the lift?" Then he thought of the way he'd moved the heavy backdrops off his dad. All he needed was enough leverage.

He left his dad snoring and headed back to the under stage area to look at the lift. The lift wheel was metal and shaped a lot like the wheels that turned to open hatches in submarine movies.

He found a long, thin piece of broken board in the area where the crates had fallen. He shoved one end of the board into the open parts of the wheel. Then he threw his full weight onto the other end. For a moment, nothing happened. The wheel was stuck. Then slowly, it began to turn.

Moving the lift plate enough to see underneath was slow work. Jack had to pull out the broken board and reposition it over and over, throwing his weight against it each time. The lift crept up by creaking inches. Finally, it was high enough for Jack to creep under it on hands and knees.

He found a round hole in the floor under the lift and a ladder leading down. Jack swung himself down onto the ladder. It reminded him of movies he'd seen of sewers. Could he have found a hidden entrance to the sewers of Dareville?

At the bottom, the floor was damp but not filled with the mucky water Jack expected. He looked around and spotted a light ahead. He trotted toward it and discovered a room with a bed, a kitchenette, and one very live actor. "Mr. Dare," Jack said.

The actor turned sharply. Without the thick ghost makeup, he looked much older. "Well, aren't you a clever boy?"

"You wanted me to solve the mystery of your disappearance," Jack said. "I think I have. You faked it and moved down here. I don't know why though."

The actor sighed. "I knew the theater was dying. I wanted to go out on top. If I'd stayed, I would have ended up selling diet aids on television in the middle of the night like that horrible Felix Marshall." Dare laughed. "He showed the world his greatness all right. He is a sad huckster. And I am the great actor who vanished onstage."

Jack put his hands on his hips and glared. "Why did you arrange those accidents for me and my dad? One of us could have been killed."

"I did not. Those truly were accidents. The caretakers of that fine old theater have taken dreadful care, and it's falling apart. At first, that's why I haunted them. I hoped to get rid of the lazy ones so someone would come in and do a good job. But they've all been the same. The only good thing to come of my little haunting has been spreading my legend."

"There's one thing I haven't been able to figure out," Jack said. "How did you float down to save me when I fell through the trapdoor?"

The ghost grinned. "Classic misdirection and precise planning. I stood in the exact spot I needed you to stand so that you would fall, but have time to catch yourself. While you were in your predicament, I simply snapped a cable to a harness I wore under my clothes. Then I could lower myself down exactly like Peter Pan flew so long ago on that very stage."

"Why go to all this trouble? Why did you ask me to solve the mystery in the first place?" Jack asked.

"To keep it alive, my boy. I never imagined you'd find the real answer. I can't have that. I would lose my home. Worse yet, I would lose my legend. I've worked so hard with my projectors and mirrors and secret cables. I can't have it all come out. I'm afraid you'll have to stay down here until I figure out something more permanent."

"Not likely." Jack stuck his hand into his pocket and pulled out the can of salt. He flung the contents into Dare's face. The actor howled as the salt crystals stung his eyes. Jack turned and ran.

He realized almost immediately that he'd run the wrong way. He wouldn't be able to get back to the ladder without passing Dare again. He just hoped he'd find another way out.

When he reached a second ladder, he could hear Dare bellowing behind him. Jack scrambled up the ladder. At the top, he flung back a trapdoor and was shocked to see he was inside a house. He scrambled to his feet just as the strange woman who'd given him the salt came into the room.

"Come out of there," she said. "I'll deal with him."

Dare scrambled out right behind Jack, but the woman stepped in front of the actor. "Forget it.

You're not going to hurt a child."

"But Emily, he'll ruin everything," Dare snapped.

She shook her head. "I've called the police. I did it as soon as I heard the ruckus under the floor. The time for scaring folks is over."

"They deserved it," Dare snapped. "They didn't take care of the theater."

"My dad will," Jack said. "You didn't give him a chance, but he'll do a good job. He'll take care of the place."

Dare's shoulders slumped. "I suppose that will have to be enough."

They heard sirens in the distance and the woman took Dare's hand. "You're the greatest actor I ever saw. But it's time for the show to be over."

The old actor nodded, then turned to look at Jack. "It is better to learn wisdom late than never to learn it at all."

Jack recognized the Sherlock Holmes quote, so he added one of his own, slightly changed.

"My name is Jack. It is my business to know what other people don't know."

Dare chuckled softly. "Clever boy."

With that, they shuffled out to greet the arriving police cars.

ENDING
→ 3 ←

Forever Lonely

The fancy cursive writing on the note had been hard to understand in places, so Jack reread it carefully.

Dear Emily,

I'm stealing a moment between scenes to write this. I should just tell you, of course. Each time I have tried, I realize that I cannot look at your serious face and talk about otherworldly things. You would laugh at me. You think actors are too imaginative. But I am not laughing.

This theater has always been a welcome home for me. Coming to the dressing room for each performance is like visiting a dear friend. But not lately. Not since the owner told us that we will be shutting down by the end of the month. We simply don't draw the audience that we once did.

I know how silly this sounds, but I believe the theater is not happy. The feeling of joy is gone. There are more shadows. Everyone is jumpy. I am afraid.

Jack flipped through the pages of the book, looking for more of the letter. He guessed Dare must have been called away to the stage. He never got a chance to finish the note.

"The theater didn't want you to go," Jack whispered.

"No, it did not."

Jack turned to face the ghost of Victor Dare. The ghost's shoulders were slumped and his face more lined than before. "What happened?" Jack asked.

"It's so odd. I remember now," Dare said. "It began with a series of little accidents. They could all be explained by the age of the building."

Jack's eyes widened. "Accidents like crates and backdrops falling?"

"Different, but much like that," the ghost agreed. "Until the night of my last show, and the greatest accident of all."

"That trapdoor."

Dare nodded. "I fell through, but I never landed. I simply fell and fell and fell. I can still feel myself falling. I imagine I always will. The theater trapped me at that moment of falling. No one ever saw me alive again."

"I'm sorry," Jack said.

"So am I." The ghost looked at Jack with eyes full of sadness. "I didn't remember. I would have told you to run. I would have warned you."

"Warned me about what?" Jack asked.

"The theater closed. I wasn't enough company," the ghost said. "The theater wants the company, you see? It wants all the company it can get. That's why the caretakers never leave."

"That's what the accidents have been about?" Jack asked, panic making his stomach sick. "The theater is trying to kill my dad and me?"

"It's just lonely. It can't stand being lonely."

Jack didn't care about the theater's loneliness. He had to get his dad and get out while they still could. He dashed out the door of the dressing room and ran for the stairs.

"Be careful!" Dare shouted after him. "I'm not the only ghost!"

When Jack reached the stairway to the basement, he skidded to a shocked stop. A small crowd of ghosts stood between him and the stairs. The ghosts were all men in rough clothes and grim faces. They began shuffling toward him.

"Don't let them touch you! They belong to the theater now."

As he backed up, Jack turned to see the lined face of the woman from next door. "What are you doing here?"

"Getting you out while you still can," she said.

"I have to get to my dad!" Jack wailed, backing up desperately as the ghosts continued to advance.

"Use the salt," she urged.

Jack pulled the can of salt from the pocket on his hoodie. He opened it with shaking fingers. The ghosts shuffled still closer, arms extended toward him. He flung salt on the ghosts. As soon as the crystals hit, the ghosts began to shrivel up like slugs. Soon they were nothing but sticky puddles on the floor.

"Now get your father!" the woman shouted. "Hurry!"

Jack raced down the stairs to the apartment. He threw open the door. His father was still asleep on the sofa, snoring softly. Jack shook him. "Dad, wake up!"

His dad's eyes opened. He blinked at Jack. "What? Is something wrong?"

"Yes, it's an emergency," Jack said. "We have to get out of the theater."

His dad quickly scrambled to his feet. "What's wrong? Is it a fire?"

"I'll tell you outside," Jack insisted. To his surprise, his dad didn't argue. Instead he grabbed Jack's hand, and they ran for the stairs. As soon as they stepped onto the staircase, it began to shake and buck under their feet.

His dad grabbed the railing. "Is it an earthquake?"

"We just have to get out."

Jack heard a crack as loud as a gunshot. Another followed. He looked over the side of the stairs and saw two of the big support columns in the basement cracking. His dad must have seen the same, because he tugged Jack up the stairs at a run.

They ran for the stage door, dodging debris that fell all around them. Hunks of wood and plaster dropped out of the ceiling. Beams suddenly punched through the walls. Each time, Jack's dad ducked and twisted and pulled Jack past the danger.

"Hurry! Hurry!" Up ahead, the woman stood at the open stage door. The light from the door shone on her oddly, making her seem almost transparent.

Suddenly the floor rolled under their feet. Holes opened ahead of them. Jack's dad grabbed him completely off his feet and jumped over the holes. They dashed outside.

"Keep running!" the woman shouted after them. "Run clear!"

"You too," Jack's dad said, holding out a hand to her. She shook her head and backed into the theater. As they watched, the years seemed to fall away from the woman's face, leaving someone young and lovely.

"Victor is waiting for me," she said. "You go now. Go fast."

Jack's dad didn't argue. They raced to the far edge of the parking lot. They turned to look back as the theater fell in upon itself until nothing was left but rubble and swirling dust. For an instant, the dust seemed to take the shape of a man and a woman standing close together. Then it simply fell to the ground.

Jack and his father had to answer a lot of questions. None of Jack's answers included ghosts. No one would believe him. It was enough that he had solved the mystery. It was enough that he knew the truth.

WRITE YOUR OWN ENDING

There were three endings to choose from in *Ghost Light Burning*. Did you find the ending you wanted from the story? Or did you want something different to happen? Now it is your turn! Write the ending you would like to see. Be creative!